I am a Ballerina

Written by Valerie Coulman

Illustrated by Sandra Lamb

Lobster Press ™

I am a Ballerina
Text © 2004 Valerie Coulman
Illustrations © 2004 Sandra Lamb

Published in 2005 by Lobster Press™
1620 Sherbrooke Street West, Suites C & D
Montréal, Québec   H3H 1C9
Tel. (514) 904-1100 • Fax (514) 904-1101
www.lobsterpress.com

Publisher: Alison Fripp
Editors: Alison Fripp & Karen Li
Graphic Design & Production: Tammy Desnoyers

We acknowledge the financial support of the Government of Canada through the Book Publishing Industry Development Program (BPIDP) for our publishing activities.

We acknowledge the support of
the Canada Council for the Arts
for our publishing program.

Library and Archives Canada Cataloguing in Publication

Coulman, Valerie, 1969-
     I am a ballerina / Valerie Coulman ; illustrated by Sandra Lamb.

ISBN 1-894222-91-1 (bound).-ISBN 1-897073-20-8 (pbk.)

     I. Lamb, Sandra, 1958- II. Title.

PS8555.O82295I2 2004   C813'.6   C2004-901088-3

Printed and bound in Canada.

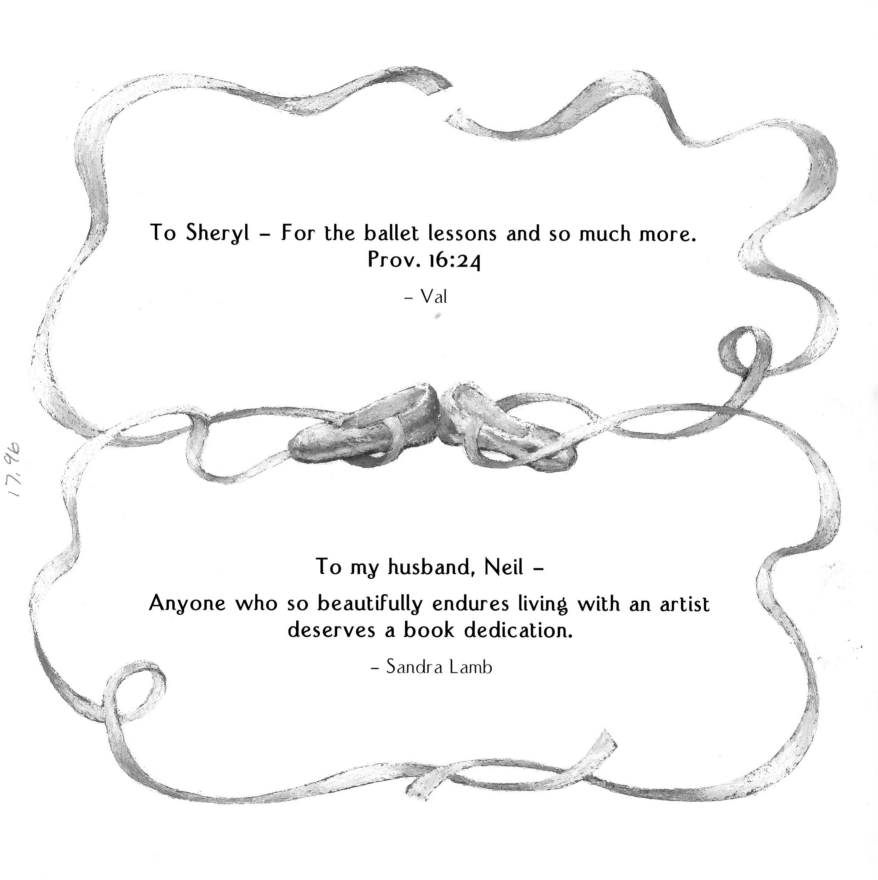

To Sheryl – For the ballet lessons and so much more.
Prov. 16:24

– Val

To my husband, Neil –

Anyone who so beautifully endures living with an artist deserves a book dedication.

– Sandra Lamb

I am a ballerina.

Well, almost a ballerina.

For my birthday Mom took me to see the ballet. We sat in the dark in a big theatre while beautiful dancers sparkled in and out of the lights on the stage.

Sometimes the music was very quiet and the dancers would tiptoe around. Sometimes the music was very loud and the dancers would jump and spin. Once the prince even lifted the princess high in the air! It looked like she was flying.

When they finished, I clapped and clapped until my hands tingled.

I told Mom, "I am going to be a ballerina."

Mom said,
"Is that right, dear?"

"I can jump high in the air.
See?"

Dad said,
"Jump down, dear."

"I can spin on my toes like a ballerina. See?"

Dad laughed. "If you're going to be a ballerina, maybe you should take some lessons."

At Madame Cherie's School of Dance, I could see myself everywhere! There were long mirrors on the wall where I learned to hold the barre and point my toes. "Only the tip of your toe on the floor," Madame Cherie's reflection showed us.

The floor was so shiny that when I looked down, I could see myself between the tips of my pink shoes. "Stand tall and keep your chin up," Madame Cherie said.

Every week Madame Cherie taught us something new.

I learned how to hold my hands.
Madame Cherie called it
"pretty hands."

It's hard to make your bed with pretty hands.

Madame Cherie taught us five
different positions.

I seemed to know six.

I asked Madame Cherie who would lift me. She said, "No one. You won't learn that until you are much older."

That worried me just a little. Could I be a ballerina without being lifted? Teddy couldn't hold me up at all.

At the end of the lessons, Madame Cherie said we were going to dance for our parents at a recital. We were going to be horses in a merry-go-round!

We practiced and practiced.

I practiced and practiced.

On the day of the recital, Mom helped me get into my costume.
"What a wonderful costume," she said.

It was.

"My, don't you look beautiful!" Dad said.

I did.

When the music started to play, we danced onto the stage. I tiptoed when the music was quiet and spun on my toes when the music was loud. And even though I held my chin high, I could see my costume sparkling as I twirled and pranced in and out of the lights.

After we were finished, Mom clapped and laughed and smiled her proud-of-you smile.

Dad spun me around, then lifted me high in the air. "Look at you!" he said, twirling me around.

It felt like I was flying. And then I knew...

I am a ballerina.